The A to Z

Dinosaur Joke Book

From **Allosaurus** to **Zuniceratops**!

Illustrated by Vasco Icuza

Kane Miller
A DIVISION OF EDC PUBLISHING

CACKLE!
HAH!
BWAHAHA!
HAHAHA!
CHORTLE!
GIGGLE!
HE HE!
TEE-HEE!
HA HA!
LOL!

The A to Z Dinosaur Joke Book

If you're eager for roar-some jokes,
and love nothing more than hearing a tyranno-chorus
of laughter, then this is the perfect book for you!

The A to Z Dinosaur Joke Book is a sidesplitting
collection of over 300 prehistoric-themed one-liners.
The jokes are ordered alphabetically, so you can
chuckle your way from A to Z, or search for a joke
about your favorite dinosaur. From an amusing
allosaurus to zany zuniceratops, the laughs don't stop!

The A to Z Dinosaur Joke Book will provide
you with a host of dino-mite jokes!

Q Why did T. rex's short arms make it an **AFFECTIONATE** dinosaur?

A Because it had to hold everything close to its heart!

Q What came **AFTER** the dinosaur?

A Its tail!

Q Did you hear about the pianist who was eaten by an **ALLOSAURUS**?

A He was a Jurassic-ally trained musician!

CACKLE!

Q Where did the **ANCIENT** rodent Josephoartigasia live?

A In a really cool mouse pad!

Q What did dinosaurs have that no other **ANIMALS** ever had?

A Baby dinosaurs!

Q How do you **ANNOY** an Archaeopteryx?

A Ruffle its feathers!

HE HE!

Q What do you call an **ANXIOUS** dinosaur?

A A nervous rex!

Q Why did the **APATOSAURUS** devour the factory?

A Because it was a plant eater!

Q How do we know that Stegosauruses had hearty **APPETITES**?

A They always cleaned their plates!

Q What does an **ARCHAEOLOGIST** call a really old dinosaur joke?

A Pre-hysterical!

Q Why did the **ARCHAEOPTERYX** catch the worm?

A Because it was an early bird!

Q What do you call an extremely big **ARGENTINOSAURUS**?

A An Extra-large-osaurus!

Q Why were the paleontologists always **ARGUING**?

A They had a bone to pick with each other!

SNICKER!

Q How did cavemen survive the **ASTEROID** that killed all the dinosaurs?

A By social distancing—they stayed 56 million years apart!

Q What was the first thing the Allosaurus **ATE** after having its teeth cleaned?

A The dentist!

Q What's the best way to raise a **BABY** dinosaur?

A With a crane!

Q Which dinosaur likes to shop for **BARGAINS**?

A The *Megalo*saurus!

GUFFAW!

Q Why did the dinosaur bring string to the **BASEBALL** game?

A It wanted to tie the score!

Q What do you call a dinosaur that refuses to **BATHE**?

A A Stink-o-saurus!

Q Why can't you hear a Pterosaur using the **BATHROOM**?

A Because the P is silent!

Q How do you know if there's a dinosaur under your **BED**?

A Your nose hits the ceiling!

Q What do you call a dinosaur with a **BELL** tied around its neck?

A A dead ringer!

Q How do dinosaurs pay their **BILLS**?

A With Tyrannosaurus checks!

Q What do you call a **BLIND** dinosaur?

A A Do-you-think-he-saurus!

Q What should you do if you find a **BLUE** Ichthyosaur?

A Cheer him up!

HAW-HAW!

Q Were Triceratops known to be **BOASTFUL** dinosaurs?

A Yes, they were always tooting their own horns!

Q Why are there old dinosaur **BONES** in the museum?

A Because they can't afford new ones!

Q How did the massive dinosaur do in the **BOXING** ring?

A It became the heavyweight chomp!

Q Why was the **BRACHIOSAURUS** always swinging its tail?

A Because there was no one else to swing it for it!

Q Which dinosaur always eats pancakes for **BREAKFAST**?

A The Tri-syrup-tops!

LOL!

B

BWAHAHA!

Q What do you call a dinosaur after a **BREAKUP**?

A A Tyrannosaurus ex!

Q What do you call a dinosaur made up of plastic **BRICKS**?

A A Lego-saurus!

Q Why did the **BRONTOSAURUS** have a long neck?

A Because its feet really stunk!

Q What do you call a dinosaur that refuses to eat anything other than **BUSHES**?

A A hedge-atarian!

Q How do we know that Stegosauruses were really **BUSY** dinosaurs?

A They had a lot on their plates!

Q What do you **CALL** a dinosaur with a foul mouth?

A A Bronto-swore-us!

Q Why are dinosaur skeletons always so **CALM**?

A Because nothing gets under their skin!

TEE-HEE!

Q What do Triceratops eat on **CAMPING** trips?

A Dino-smores!

Q What do you call a dinosaur from **CANADA**?

A Toronto-saurus Rex!

Q What do you get if you cross a dinosaur with a **CANARY**?

A A really messy cage!

Q What made the dinosaur's **CAR** stop?

A A flat Tire-annosaurus!

Q Which dinosaur loves to play **CARD** games?

A The Tyrannosaurus decks!

CHORTLE!

Q What type of tool does a prehistoric **CARPENTER** use?

A A dino-saw!

Q What do you call it when dinosaurs crash their **CARS**?

A Tyrannosaurus wrecks!

Q What do you call a **CAVEMAN** with bad posture?

A A concave man!

Q Where do dinosaurs follow **CAVEMEN**?

A In the dictionary!

Q What kind of dinosaur is made of **CHEESE**?

A The Gorgon-zilla!

Q What happened to the man who crossed a T. rex with a **CHICKEN**?

A He got a Tyrannosaurus pecks!

Q Why can't a T. rex **CLAP** its hands?

A Because it's extinct!

GIGGLE!

Q How did the dinosaurs get **CLEAN**?

A In meteor showers!

SNICKER!

Q How do you **CLONE** a dinosaur?

A Using a Photocopy-saurus!

Q What theme park **CLONED** long-necked dinosaurs?

A Giraff-ic Park!

Q Who makes the best prehistoric reptile **CLOTHES**?

A A dino-sewer!

Q Where does the dinosaur **CLOWN** work?

A At the carnivore!

Q Why couldn't the dinosaur play games on the **COMPUTER**?

A Because it ate the mouse!

Q What's the difference between a **COOKIE** and a mammoth?

A Try dunking a mammoth in your milk!

Q What do you get when you cross a Stegosaurus with a **COW**?

A Milk that's scary to drink!

GUFFAW!

Q Which dinosaur did the **COWBOY** try to ride?

A The Bronco-saurus!

Q What has a prominent head **CREST**, a duck-like bill, and eight wheels?

A A Parasaurolophus on roller skates!

Q Which dinosaur could put a **CURSE** on you?

A The Tyrannosaurus hex!

15

CHUCKLE!

Q What happened when two ferocious dinosaurs went on a blind **DATE**?

A It was love at first bite!

Q What do you call the prehistoric **DENTIST** who fixed dinosaurs' teeth?

A Really brave!

Q What should you do when a dinosaur starts to eat your **DICTIONARY**?

A Take the words right out of its mouth!

Q How do you stop a stinky **DILOPHOSAURUS** from smelling?

A Plug its nostrils!

Q Which dinosaurs were always popular guests at **DINNER** parties?

A Stegosauruses—they brought their own plates!

Q Why was it smelly near the **DINOSAURS'** nest?

A Because their eggs stink!

Q What's better than a talking **DIPLODOCUS**?

A A spelling bee!

Q Which dinosaur never had to ask for **DIRECTIONS**?

A The Mapusaurus!

Q What do you call a **DOG** that sniffs rocks and barks when it finds a dinosaur fossil?

A A professional bark-eologist!

Q How do you get **DOWN** from a dinosaur?

A You don't—you get down from a goose!

HAW-HAW!

GIGGLE!

Q What is a poorly **DRESSED** dinosaur called?

A An eye-saur!

Q How do you ask a Tyrannosaur if they'd like a hot **DRINK**?

A "Tea, Rex?"

Q What kind of fuel do dinosaurs use to **DRIVE** their cars?

A Fossil fuels!

Q What should you do if a dinosaur starts **DRIVING** your car?

A Not stand in its way!

Q Did the young **DRYPTOSAURUS** look like its parents?

A Yep—it was a dryp off the old block!

18

Q Which **EARLY** humans led a nomadic lifestyle?

A The meander-thals!

Q Why don't we see dinosaurs at **EASTER**?

A Because they are eggs-tinct!

Q Why was the Tyrannosaurus such a good **ECONOMIST**?

A Because it excelled at crunching numbers!

Q How many Sauropods can you fit in an **EMPTY** box?

A One—after that the box is no longer empty!

Q Why did the **EUOPLOCEPHALUS** say "knock, knock"?

A Because it was in the wrong joke book!

WAHAHA

19

Q Which no longer **EXISTING** big cat didn't order dessert?

A The savory-toothed tiger!

Q What kind of dinosaur used to **EXPLODE** suddenly?

A The Tricera-pops!

Q What kind of **EXPLOSIONS** do dinosaurs like?

A Dino-mite ones!

Q What comes after **EXTINCT**?

A Y-stinct!

GUFFAW!

Q What do you call a meteor that causes an **EXTINCTION** event?

A A disaster-oid!

Q Why should you never take a dinosaur bone on a **FAIRGROUND** roller coaster?

A It'll jostle your fossil!

HAH!

Q What **FAMILY** does Velociraptor belong to?

A I don't know; I don't think any family in our neighborhood owns one!

Q What kind of dinosaur is helpful on a **FARM**?

A T. ractor!

Q What was the name of the **FASTEST** dinosaur?

A The Pronto-saurus!

Q Which dinosaur has the best time on **FATHER'S** Day?

A The Tricera-pops!

F

Q What is a dinosaur's **FAVORITE** cheese?

A Roar-quefort!

CACKLE!

Q What's big, **FEATHERY**, and bounces?

A An Archaeopteryx on a trampoline!

Q What do guests wipe their **FEET** on when entering Diplodocus's cave?

A The diplomat!

Q What do fossil **FINDERS** spread on their toast?

A Preserves!

Q Where can you find fossils of the very **FIRST** cows?

A At the Moo-seum of Natural History!

Q What do you call a mammoth that **FLIES**?

A A jumbo jet!

Q How do you make a dinosaur **FLOAT**?

A Put a scoop of ice cream in a glass of root beer and add a dinosaur!

Q Were mammoths easy to **FOOL**?

A Yes—you could pull the wool over their eyes!

Q Why did the referee kick the Ankylosaurus out of the **FOOTBALL** game?

A It kept spiking the ball!

TEE-HEE!

Q What type of **FOOTWEAR** do basketball-playing dinosaurs like?

A Tricera-high-tops!

Q Why don't dinosaurs ever **FORGET** anything?

A Because no one tells them anything!

CHORTLE!

Q What kind of music do **FOSSIL** records play?

A Hard rock!

Q Why is it hard to make **FOSSIL HUNTERS** laugh?

A They don't find jokes humerus!

Q Where can you find **FOSSILS** of dinosaur snakes?

A At the Museum of Natural Hissss-tory!

Q When were dinosaurs at their most **FRIENDLY**?

A During the nice age!

Q What do you call a dinosaur with **GAS**?

A A blast from the past!

Q What do you call a dinosaur **GHOST**?

A A Scary-dactyl!

Q What does a **GIANT** Tyrannosaurus eat?

A Anything it wants!

Q What's the best dinosaur to help with **GIFTS**?

A A Veloci-wrap-tor!

HAHAHA!

Q What is **GIGANOTOSAURUS'** favorite ice-skating move?

A The figure ate!

Q What's worse than a **GIRAFFE** with a cough?

A A Diplodocus with a sore throat!

Q Which early humans had a very healthy **GLOW**?

A The Neon-derthals!

Q What do you call it when a dinosaur kicks a **GOAL** with a soccer ball?

A A dino-score!

Q Which dinosaur loved to play **GOLF**?

A The Tee rex!

Q What do you do with a **GREEN** dinosaur?

A Wait until it ripens!

HA HA!

Q What do you call a woolly mammoth after a **HAIRCUT**?

A A not-so-woolly mammoth!

Q What do you call a flying dinosaur that uses its **HANDS** to see?

A A Tactile-dactyl!

Q What kind of dinosaur would **HARRY POTTER** be?

A A Dino-sorcerer!

Q When is the best time for dinosaur eggs to **HATCH**?

A At the crack of dawn!

Q What do you call a prehistoric big cat wearing wireless **HEADPHONES**?

A A cyber-toothed tiger!

H

Q What happens to a fossil in a **HEAVY** thunderstorm?

A It gets soaked to the bone!

Q What do you call a dinosaur wearing **HIGH HEELS**?

A A My-feet-are-saurus!

Q How do Pterodactyls get ready for the **HOLIDAYS**?

A They don't, they just wing it!

Q What happened after the dinosaur took the school bus **HOME**?

A The school called and asked for it back!

Q What has eight legs, six **HORNS**, and four eyes?

A A Triceratops looking in the mirror!

HA HA!

Q Why were the paleontologists disappointed after they examined the limb of an ancient **HUMANOID** dinosaur?

A It turned out to be a fossil arm!

Q What were the ghosts of early **HUMANS** called?

A Haunter-gatherers!

Q What do you call a one **HUNDRED** dinosaur stampede?

A An earthquake!

Q What would happen if a **HUNDRED-TON** Brachiosaurus stepped on you?

A You'd be deeply impressed!

LOL!

Q What is a **HUNGRY** dinosaur's favorite day of the week?

A Chews-day!

Q How did dinosaur fossils feel at the start of the **ICE AGE**?

A Chilled to the bone!

Q What's the best thing to give a seasick **ICHTHYOSAUR**?

A Plenty of room!

Q What is **IGUANODON'S** favorite piece of playground equipment?

A The dino-see-saur!

Q What do you call a good dinosaur **IMPRESSION**?

A A roaring success!

Q Where in **ITALY** can you find mammoth fossils?

A Tusk-any!

SNICKER!

Q What do you call dinosaur **JESTERS**?

A Fossil fools!

Q What would a Dilophosaurus wear to a **JOB** interview?

A A double-crested jacket!

Q Why didn't anyone laugh at the flying dinosaur **JOKE**?

A It was Ptero-ble!

Q What do you call a Deinonychus that is fantastic at **JUGGLING**?

A Talon-ted!

HE HE!

Q What do **JUVENILE** dinosaurs do in order to hatch from eggs?

A They plan an eggs-it strategy!

Q What do you get if you cross a Triceratops with a **KANGAROO**?

A A Tricera-hops!

Q What do you call museum exhibits that show models of dinosaurs being **KILLED** by predators?

A Die-oramas!

Q Why did the dinosaur give up using a prehistoric **LAPTOP**?

A It only had one Ptero-byte of storage space!

Q Did you hear that dinosaurs hunted in **LARGE** packs?

A Yes—I herd!

Q How do you make a dinosaur fossil **LAUGH**?

A Tickle its funny bone!

GIGGLE!

HA HA!

Q Are dinosaur fossils good **LEARNERS**?

A Yes, they always keep an open mind!

Q What do you get if you cross a dinosaur with a **LEMON**?

A A dino-sour!

Q Why did **LEPTOCERATOPS** travel in packs?

A Because if they traveled in flocks they'd be mistaken for sheep!

Q Why did dinosaurs **LIE** down to sleep?

A Because they couldn't lie up!

Q How many dinosaurs did it take to change a **LIGHT BULB**?

A Only one, but they had to wait 200 million years for the light bulb to be invented!

33

Q What prehistoric animal is drawn to **LIGHTS**?

A Mam*moths*!

Q What do you call a flying prehistoric **LIZARD**?

A A dino-soaring!

CHUCKLE!

Q Do you know how **LONG** dinosaurs should be fed?

A Exactly the same way as short dinosaurs!

Q What is **LOUDER** than a dinosaur?

A A whole bunch of dinosaurs!

Q How do you describe two Allosauruses that **LOVE** each other?

A They are en-raptored!

Q Which college subject could dinosaurs never **MAJOR** in?

A History!

Q Who would prehistoric **MATADORS** battle in the ring?

A Torosaurus!

Q Which **MATERIALS** do dinosaurs use for flooring?

A Rep-tiles!

Q Why do dinosaurs eat raw **MEAT**?

A Because they don't know how to cook!

TEE-HEE!

Q Which branch of science studies **MEGALODON**, the prehistoric shark?

A Sharky-ology!

Q Who was in charge of the **MICRORAPTORS'** baseball team?

A The Micro-manager!

Q What is in the **MIDDLE** of dinosaurs?

A The letter *S*!

Q Why don't dinosaurs have **MONEY** problems?

A Because they don't have to worry about the cost of living!

Q What kind of fossils can be found in **MONGOLIA**?

A Mongolian ones!

Q What kind of mammoth loves to do stunts on a **MOTORCYCLE**?

A A wheelie mammoth!

Q What's the nickname for someone who put their right hand into the **MOUTH** of a T. rex?

A Lefty!

HAH!

Q What kind of traffic jam happens when too many Diplodocuses are on the **MOVE**?

A A massive bottleneck!

Q How do dinosaur skeletons talk to each other at the **MUSEUM**?

A On the tele-bone!

Q What **MUSIC** do dinosaurs listen to?

A Raptor music!

Q What is a Triceratops' favorite **MUSICAL** instrument?

A The horn!

Q Where did the dinosaurs go to get their **NAILS** done?

A The talon salon!

Q How did the dinosaur feel after building a **NEST**?

A Eggs-hausted!

Q What do you call a **NEWBORN** dinosaur?

A A wee rex!

Q What makes more **NOISE** than a dinosaur?

A Two dinosaurs!

Q What was T. rex's favorite **NUMBER**?

A Ate!

CACKLE!

Q Why was the dinosaur afraid of the **OCEAN**?

A Because there was something fishy about it!

Q What should you shout if an **ODONTOSAURUS** charges toward you?

A "Oh, don't!"

Q What do you call dinosaurs that **ONLY** eat pine cones?

A Cone-iferous!

Q What did the dinosaur get from the **OPTOMETRIST**?

A Tyrannosaurus specs!

Q How do you encourage an **OVIRAPTOR**?

A You egg it on!

HAHAHA!

Q What do you call a **PALEONTOLOGIST** who naps on the job?

A Lazy bones!

Q Do **PALEONTOLOGISTS** enjoy their job?

A Yes—they really dig their work!

Q What's the difference between a Pterodactyl and a **PARROT**?

A A Pterodactyl is much harder to carry around on your shoulder!

Q How were **PARTICULARLY** savage prehistoric humans described?

A Fur-ocious!

HE HE!

Q When did the dinosaurs eat lots of baked goods and **PASTRIES**?

A During the Scone Age!

Q What do you call a dinosaur that **PERSEVERES**?

A Try-try-try-ceratops!

Q What do you call a mammoth in a **PHONE** booth?

A Stuck!

Q What do you get when you cross a **PIG** with a dinosaur?

A Jurassic pork!

Q How did the dinosaur feel after he ate a **PILLOW**?

A A bit down in the mouth!

Q What do you call a **PIRATE** that digs for fossils?

A An arrrr-chaeologist!

SNICKER!

41

Q What do dinosaurs put on their **PIZZA**?

A Tomato-saurus!

HAW-HAW!

Q What do dinosaurs use to go from **PLANET** to planet?

A A flying dino-saucer!

Q Did you hear about the disastrous prehistoric **PLAY**?

A It was a real Tricera-flop!

Q What should always follow a **PLESIOSAURUS**?

A A Thank-you-a-lot-a-sus!

Q Which dinosaurs were the best **POLICE OFFICERS**?

A The Tricera-cops!

Q What do you call a **POLITE** dinosaur?

A A Please-osaur!

Q What does a dinosaur call a **PORCUPINE**?

A A toothbrush!

Q What were enormous **PREHISTORIC** pigs called?

A Swine-osaurs!

Q What's the difference between a **PTERODACTYL** and a chicken?

A No one offers you a bowl of Pterodactyl soup when you are sick!

Q What do you call a dinosaur's **PUPPY**?

A Rex!

LOL!

Q What is a dinosaur fossil's best **QUALITY**?

A Its dead-ication!

Q What do you call a prehistoric creature that has been knighted by the **QUEEN**?

A Dino-sir!

Q Did you hear about the cavemen on a **QUEST** to cook a Brachiosaur's toes?

A If successful, it'll be no small feet!

Q What do you call a dinosaur that asks a lot of deep **QUESTIONS**?

A A Philos-oraptor!

Q Which dinosaur wasn't so **QUICK**?

A Di-plod-ocus!

CHORTLE!

44

Q How did the **RACE** between the two Diplodocuses end?

A They finished neck and neck!

Q What happens to dinosaurs when it's **RAINING**?

A They get wet, just like everyone else!

Q Why didn't the T. rex **RECOGNIZE** the female Stegosaurus?

A It had never seen herbivore!

Q How can you tell if there's a Stegosaurus in your **REFRIGERATOR**?

A The door won't close!

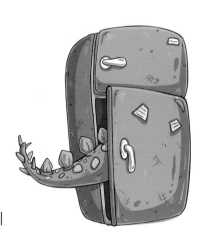

Q What do you call a dinosaur that can travel over any **REGION** on Earth?

A An All-terrain-osaurus Rex!

Q What is a dinosaur's least favorite **REINDEER**?

A Comet!

HAH!

Q How do we know that Barosauruses were **RISK** takers?

A They always stuck their necks out!

Q Why didn't the dinosaur cross the **ROAD**?

A Because roads weren't invented yet!

Q Why did the Brontosaurus let out a huge **ROAR**?

A Because it hated small talk!

Q In what **ROCKS** do we find the fossils of lazy dinosaurs?

A Sedentary rocks!

Q How do you brush a **SABER-TOOTHED** tiger's teeth?

A Very, very carefully!

Q What's a **SAILOR'S** favorite dinosaur?

A The mast-odon!

Q What **SAUCE** did the dinosaur put on its steak?

A Dino-sauce!

Q What did the **SAUROPOD** say to the Theropod?

A "Hey, wanna grab a bite?"

Q Why did **SAUROPOSEIDON**, the tallest known dinosaur, get a PhD?

A Because it was interested in higher education!

GUFFAW!

Q What is **SCARIER** than a dinosaur?

A A herd of dinosaurs!

Q What was the **SCARIEST** prehistoric animal?

A The Terror-dactyl!

Q What did the Diplodocus get when she graduated from **SCHOOL**?

A A *diplo*ma!

Q How do paleontologists **SEARCH** for Tyrannosauruses?

A On rex-peditions!

Q Which dinosaur was entirely **SIGHTLESS**?

A The Never-saur-us!

BWAHAHA!

48

Q What do you call a group of dinosaurs who **SING**?

A A Tyranno-chorus!

Q What does a Triceratops **SIT** on?

A Its Tricera-bottom!

Q Why wouldn't the dinosaur **SKELETON** attack the museum visitors?

A Because it had no guts!

Q What did the caveman say when he **SLID** down the Brachiosaurus's neck?

A "Soooo long!"

CACKLE!

Q Why was the Brachiosaurus so **SLOW** to apologize?

A It took a long time for it to swallow its pride!

Q What do you get when a dinosaur **SNEEZES**?

A Out of the way as quickly as you can!

Q What do you get when you cross a dinosaur and a **SNOWMAN**?

A Frostbite!

Q Which dinosaur likes **SPICY** food?

A The Chile-saurus!

Q What **SPORT** is a Brontosaurus best at?

A Squash!

TEE-HEE!

Q What do you call a short, spiky dinosaur who falls down the **STAIRS**?

A An Ankle-is-sore-us!

Q How do dinosaurs like their **STEAK**?

A Rawwwwwww!

Q What do you call a Tyrannosaurus rex when it's wearing a **STETSON** hat and boots?

A A Tyrannosaurus Tex!

Q What type of **STORIES** are Diplodocuses famous for?

A Long tails!

Q What happened to the **STYRACOSAURUS** who was looking for its lost neck fringe?

A It became a frill seeker!

HA HA!

Q What is Ankylosaurus's favorite **SUIT** in a deck of cards?

A Clubs!

S

Q Where was the dinosaur when the **SUN** went down?

A In the dark!

Q What did they call **SUNRISE** in prehistoric times?

A Mega-lo-dawn!

HAHAHA!

Q Why did dinosaurs **SURVIVE** longer than dragons?

A Because they didn't smoke!

Q What type of **SWEATERS** does a T. rex prefer?

A V. nex!

Q What do mammoths wear when they go **SWIMMING**?

A Their trunks!

Q What did the dinosaur call its **T-SHIRT** business?

A Try Sarah's Tops!

Q What do you get if you cross a dog and a **T. REX**?

A A very frightened letter carrier!

Q What's the best way to **TALK** to a dinosaur?

A Long distance!

LOL!

Q What do you call a Gigantoraptor that never stops **TALKING**?

A A dino-bore!

Q Why was the **TEENAGE** dinosaur so moody?

A ROAR-mones!

Q Can you name **TEN** dinosaurs in five seconds?

A Yes—nine Iguanadons and one Stegosaurus!

Q How did the paleontologists celebrate finding the largest dinosaur **TIBIA** ever?

A With a real shindig!

Q Why did the dinosaur paint her **TOENAILS** red?

A So she could hide in the strawberry patch!

Q Who gave the dinosaurs money whenever they lost a **TOOTH**?

A The Tooth Fairy-dactyl!

Q Is it true that a dinosaur won't attack if you hold a **TREE** branch?

A It depends on how quickly you run with it!

HAH!

Q What's the difference between a minivan and **TRICERATOPS**?

A A minivan only has one horn!

HE HE!

Q What's the difference between a Pterodactyl and a **TURKEY**?

A The drumsticks are much bigger on a Pterodactyl!

Q What's huge and shaggy with **TUSKS** and horns?

A The Woolly Mammoth Marching Band!

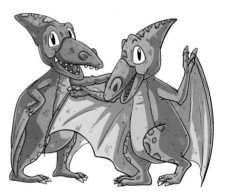

Q What do you call **TWIN** dinosaurs?

A Pair-odactyls!

Q What makes a **TYRANNO-SORE**?

A Too much rex-ercise!

Q When can two dinosaurs use only one **UMBRELLA** and not get wet?

A When it's not raining!

GIGGLE!

Q What do you call it when an archaeologist **UNCOVERS** the bones of a dinosaur's head?

A Skullduggery!

Q Which dinosaur loved to ride **UNDERGROUND** trains?

A Di*metro*don!

Q What does a paleontologist do to collect **UNHATCHED** dinosaurs?

A Eggs-cavate!

Q What did the **UNLUCKY**-in-love paleontologist sign up for?

A Carbon dating!

Q Which **UPRIGHT** early human lived near a volcano?

A Homo-eruptus!

Q Which dinosaur was often **UPSET**?

A Cry-ceratops!

Q What do you get if you turn a dinosaur **UPSIDE DOWN?**

A A Triceratops-y turvy!

Q Which dinosaur **USED** an ointment from a plant to treat its sunburn?

A The Aloe-saurus!

HA HA!

Q Why did the **UTAHRAPTOR** love to eat automobiles?

A Because it was a carnivore!

Q Where do prehistoric reptiles like to go on **VACATION**?

A To the dino-shore!

Q What do you call a **VAIN** Allosaurus?

A A Shallow-saurus!

Q What do you call a dinosaur that eats all of its **VEGETABLES**?

A A Broccoli-saurus!

Q Which dinosaur rode a three-wheeled **VEHICLE**?

A The Tricycle-tops!

Q Where did **VELOCIRAPTOR** buy things?

A At the dino-store!

HAHAHA!

Q What does a prehistoric **VETERINARIAN** help to heal?

A Dino-sores!

Q What do you call a dinosaur with a big **VOCABULARY**?

A A Thesaurus!

Q Which dinosaur sings in the highest **VOCAL** range?

A The Soprano-saurus rex!

Q What did the dinosaur say when it saw a **VOLCANO** erupt?

A "It's going to be a lava-ly day!"

Q Why was the Stegosaurus such a good **VOLLEYBALL** player?

A It could really spike the ball!

W

Q What has a **WAND**, wings, and brings money to woolly mammoths?

A The tusk fairy!

Q Which supplement kept **WATER-BASED** prehistoric creatures healthy?

A Vitamin Sea!

BWAHAHA!

Q What type of headgear does a dinosaur skeleton **WEAR**?

A A kneecap!

Q Why was the dinosaur **WEARING** green socks?

A Its red ones were in the wash!

Q What's the difference between an injured mammoth and bad **WEATHER**?

A One roars with pain and the other pours with rain!

Q How much does a dinosaur **WEIGH**?

A It depends on its scales!

Q What's as big as a dinosaur but **WEIGHS** nothing?

A Its shadow!

Q What has three horns and four **WHEELS**?

A A Triceratops on a skateboard!

Q What does a T. rex do **WHEN** it takes you to lunch?

A First it pours salt on your head. Then it gets out its fork!

Q What do paleontologists call the remains of the **WIDEST** dinosaur in history?

A A colossal fossil!

LOL!

Q What do you call a dinosaur that hates not **WINNING**?

A A dino-sore loser!

CHORTLE!

Q Which dinosaur tried to become a **WIZARD**?

A Diplo-hocus-pocus!

Q Which dinosaur had a **WOODEN** leg?

A The Peg-osaurus!

Q Why did the **WOOLLY** mammoth cross the road?

A Because they didn't have chickens during the Ice Age!

Q What **WORDS** do you use to scold a naughty woolly mammoth?

A "Tusk, tusk!"

Q What do paleontologist call dinosaur dental **X-RAYS**?

A Tooth pics!

HAHAHA!

Q What is the best thing to do if you see a **XENOCERATOPS**?

A Hope it doesn't see you!

Q Why are dinosaurs so scared to go on **YACHTS**?

A They are worried about ship rex!

Q Which dinosaur loves **YOGA**?

A The Tyrannosaurus flex!

Q How do you know if there is a **ZUNICERATOPS** in your bed?

A It has a *Z* embroidered on its pajamas!

LOL!

CACKLE!

HE HE!

HA HA!

BWAHAHA!

First American Edition 2022
Kane Miller, A Division of EDC Publishing
Copyright © Green Android Ltd 2022
Illustrated by Vasco Icuza

For information contact:
Kane Miller, A Division of EDC Publishing
5402 S 122nd E Ave
Tulsa, OK 74146
www.kanemiller.com
www.myubam.com

Library of Congress Control Number: 2022930112

Printed and bound in Malaysia, June 2022
ISBN: 978-1-68464-512-1